Adrift

written by Heidi E.Y. Stemple
illustrated by Anastasia Suvorova

An imprint of Interlink Publishing Group, Inc.
www.interlinkbooks.com

One tiny mouse
on one tiny boat
pitched back and forth,
adrift on the churning seas.

The sea was vast
and angry,
and the darkest green Little Mouse had ever seen.

He tried to hoist his sail.
But the wind was too strong.

He tried to drop his anchor.
But the ocean was too deep.

He felt more than a little scared.
And he felt very alone.

The sun set and Little Mouse slept fitfully.
The moon peaked in and out
from behind the gray clouds in the gray sky.

One lonely star blinked.
Little Mouse wished on it.
"Please," he said quietly. "Please."

The sun came up slowly
and without fanfare,
lighting the clouds from behind.

A clap of lightning shook the little boat.
Little Mouse hid his eyes
and counted to ten.

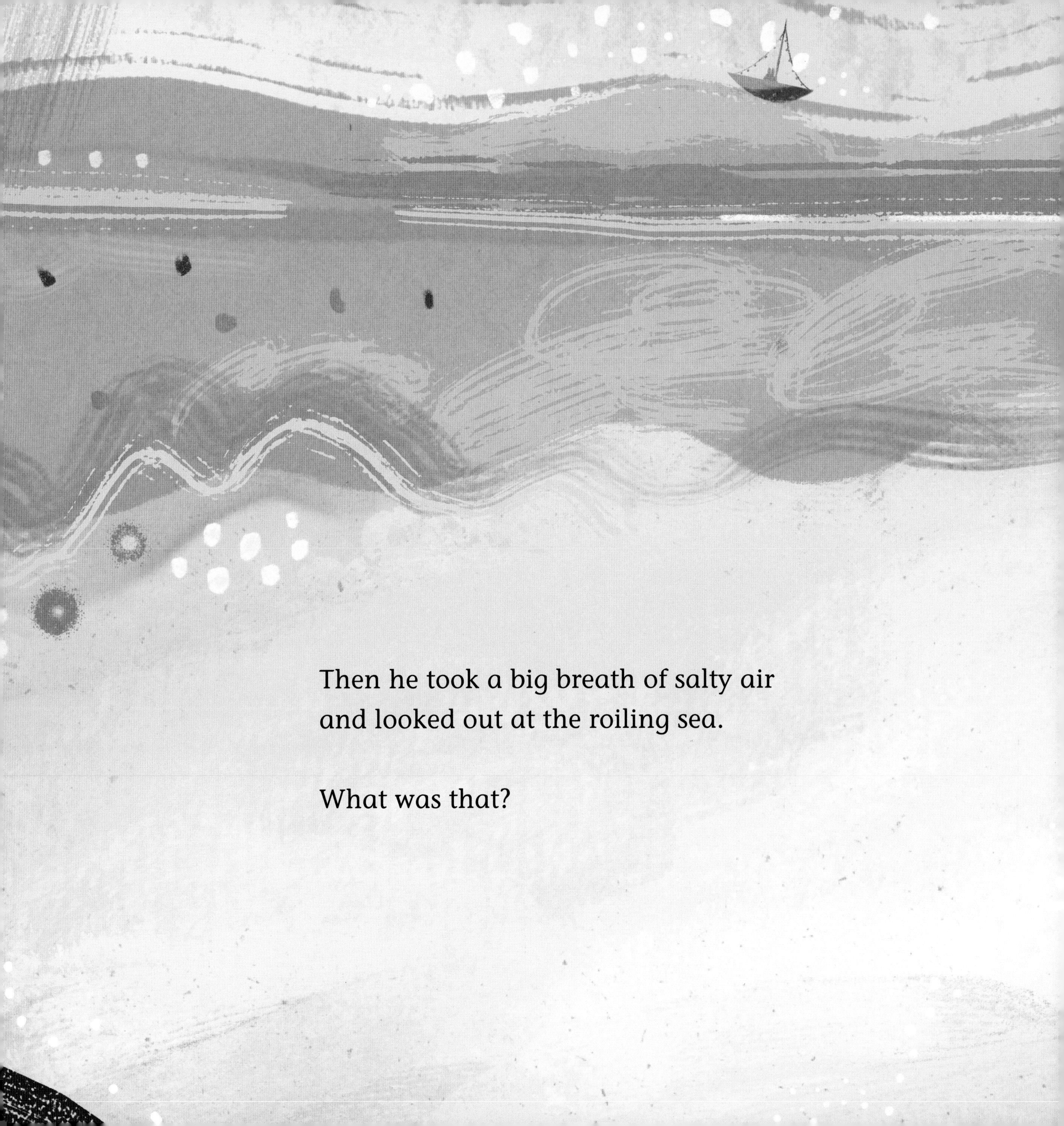

Then he took a big breath of salty air
and looked out at the roiling sea.

What was that?

Like a smudge on the horizon, something came into Little Mouse's view.

A boat! Another boat!

Little Mouse lifted his spyglass.
The other boat dipped up and down
with the waves—in and out of Little Mouse's view.

It grew bigger and bigger
as it neared Little Mouse's boat.

“Hellooooo!” Came a voice across the choppy water.
“Hellooooo!” Little Mouse called back.

The two boats bobbed in the waves
close enough to see each other, but not close enough to crash.

Little Mouse still felt more than a little afraid,
but he didn't feel quite so alone.

"Look!" yelled the other boat captain,
pointing through the rain.

Another boat was approaching.
And another, and another,
and another.

The ocean pitched the boats up and down and side to side.
The rain hit their decks, thunder boomed, and lightning cracked.
Little Mouse was still more than a little afraid,
and he was still alone on his boat.

But, even when it grew dark, the other boats were there—
close enough to feel them near, but not close enough to crash.
Little Mouse didn't feel alone at all.

Finally, the seas calmed and the wind quieted.
At the very edge of the water,
the sky blossomed peach, then yellow, then pink and purple.
Little Mouse breathed in a huge breath of salty air
and sighed it out again as the sun burst from below the horizon.

He looked around at all the other boats.

They weren't together, but they weren't alone.

A voice danced across the gently rocking water.
"Land ho!"
Little Mouse and the others raised their spyglasses,
then their sails.

One by one and side by side,
each boat anchored in the shallows.
Little mouse climbed overboard
and waded to shore where he was joined by the others.

The storm had passed.
They had survived.
And it was time to be together.

For my mother Jane and my daughter Maddison—in their own boats in this same storm. And the two beautiful friends who helped make this a book: Nina before the story and Hannah after. — H. E. Y. S.

First published in 2021 by

Crocodile Books
An imprint of Interlink Publishing Group, Inc.
46 Crosby Street, Northampton, MA 01060
www.interlinkbooks.com

Library of Congress Cataloging-in-Publication Data:
Names: Stemple, Heidi E. Y., author. | Suvorova, Anastasia, illustrator.
Title: Adrift / Heidi E.Y. Stemple ; illustrated by Anastasia Suvorova.
Description: Northampton, MA : Crocodile Books, an imprint of Interlink Publishing Group, Inc., 2021. | Audience: Ages 3-8 | Audience: Grades K-1 |
Summary: In this metaphor for the global pandemic and the power of community, a mouse in a small boat finds comfort and strength during a storm when he sees another boat and is joined by others, close enough to see each other, but not close enough to crash.
Identifiers: LCCN 2021021734 | ISBN 9781623719098 (hardback)
Subjects: CYAC: Mice--Fiction. | Boats and boating--Fiction. |
Storms--Fiction. | Community life--Fiction.
Classification: LCC PZ7.1.S7436 Ad 2021 | DDC [E]--dc23
LC record available at https://lccn.loc.gov/2021021734

Printed and bound in Korea

2 4 6 8 10 9 7 5 3 1

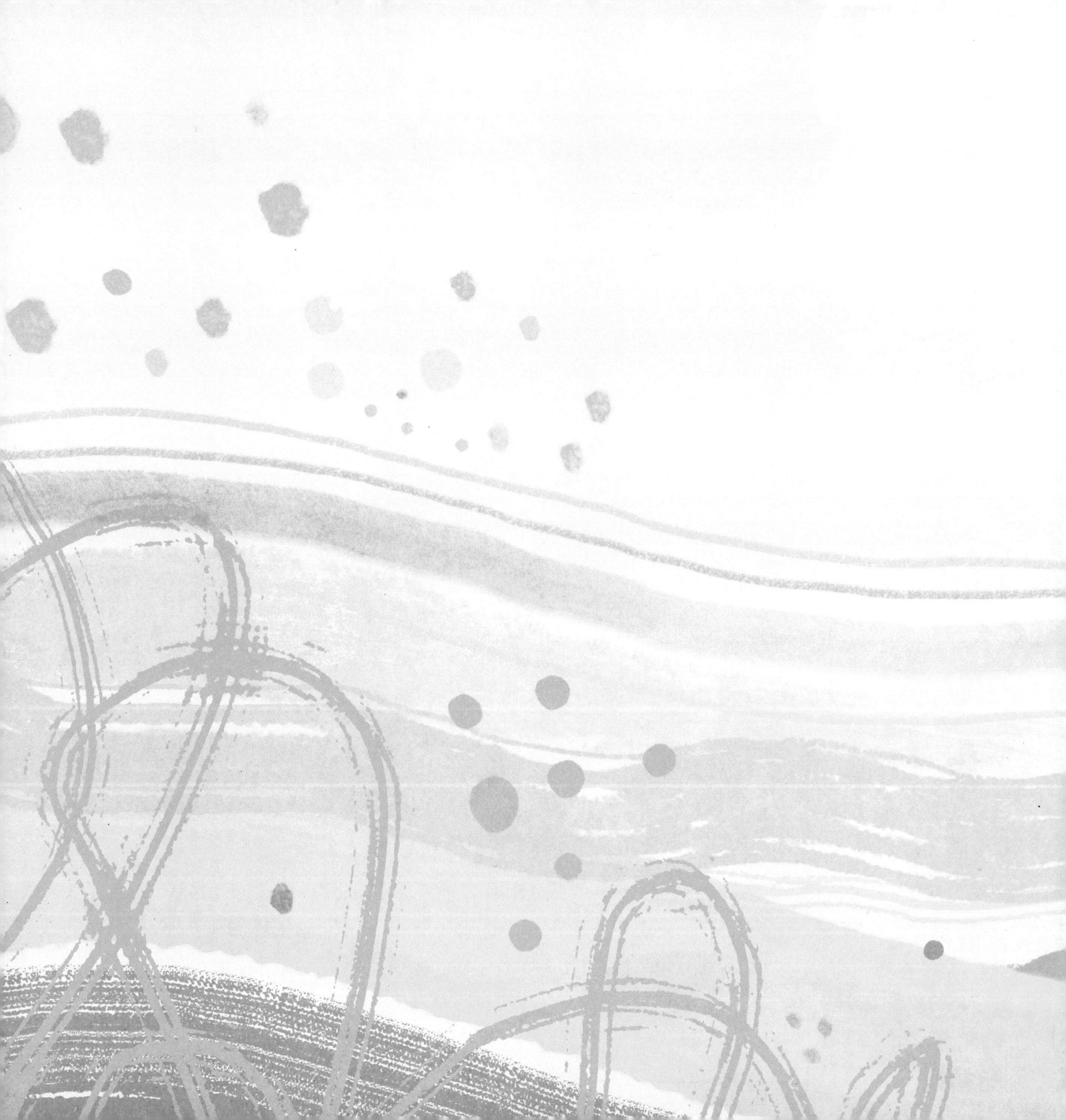